PiPeR REeD
Navy Brat

KIMBERLY WILLIS HOLT

PiPER REED

Navy BRat

Illustrated by
CHRISTINE DAVENIER

SQUARE
FISH

HENRY HOLT AND COMPANY

THANK YOU to Christy Ottaviano, Amy Berkower, Lola
Schaefer, Jeanette Ingold, Rebecca Kai Dotlich, Kathi Appelt,
Shannon Holt, Lisa Coghlan, Patrick Nichols, the Blue Angels,
the Blue Angels Elementary School, Jamason Fowler (who wanted
to spread "Get off the bus" around the world).

SQUARE
FISH

An Imprint of Macmillan

Library of Congress Cataloging-in-Publication Data
Holt, Kimberly Willis.
Piper Reed, Navy brat / Kimberly Willis Holt ; illustrated by Christine Davenier.
    p.   cm.
Summary: Piper is sad about leaving her home and friends behind when her father, a Navy aircraft
mechanic, is transferred yet again, but with help from her often-annoying sisters and a surprise
from their parents, she finds happiness in their new home in Pensacola, Florida.
ISBN: 978-0-312-38020-5
[1. Moving, Household—Fiction. 2. Sisters—Fiction. 3. Family life—Fiction. 4. Schools—Fiction.
5. United States. Navy—Fiction. 6. Pensacola (Fla.)—Fiction.] I. Davenier, Christine, ill. II. Title.
PZ7.H74023Pip 2007   [Fic]—dc22   2006035467

Originally published in the United States by Henry Holt and Company
Square Fish logo designed by Filomena Tuosto
First Square Fish Edition: 2008
10 9 8 7 6 5 4 3
www.squarefishbooks.com

For my mom, Brenda Willis,
who made every port a home

—K.W.H.

CONTENTS

PiPeR REeD
Navy Brat

1

PePsi-CoLa, FLORiDa

It was pizza night. Every Friday night, Chief picked up two large pepperoni pizzas on his way home from the base. I had just pulled the cheese off my slice and was about to put the pepperoni back on when Chief tapped a spoon against his glass of sweet tea.

Ting, ting, ting. "Girls, I have an announcement to make."

"Are we going to get a dog?" I asked.

Chief grinned, and then shook his head.

"We've been assigned to Pensacola, Florida."

Chief always said "we" when he talked about being assigned somewhere even though *he* was really the only person in the family being assigned to a new base. He would say, "When a man joins the Navy, his family joins the Navy."

That's because every year or two we had to pick up and move. I've lived everywhere. Well, almost everywhere. Before we moved to San Diego, we lived in Texas, Guam, Mississippi, and New Hampshire.

Everyone in my fourth-grade class called me Piper Reed, Navy Brat. I didn't mind, but my big sister, Tori, who was in the seventh grade, did. In fact, she didn't want Chief to be in the Navy. She wouldn't even call him Chief. She called him Dad.

"Pensacola?" Tori looked like her eyes were going to pop out of their sockets.

"When?" I asked.

"Two weeks from today," Chief said.

"Two weeks!" cried Tori. "It's only October. We've never moved during the school year!"

We always moved in the summer. That gave us a chance to make some friends before school started. Suddenly I felt like a fish was swimming around in my belly.

Tori pushed her plate away. "The Navy is ruining my life!"

"Tori," Mom said, "stop being dramatic. Everything will be fine."

"Where's Pepsi-Cola?" asked my little sister, Sam.

Mom smiled. "In Florida. Now, finish your pizza and I'll show you where Pensacola is on the map."

When we moved here, Mom had tacked a great big map of the world on the back studio wall. She said, "You're children of the world. You might as well get to know it."

"I don't want to eat my pizza," said Sam.

"I don't want to move," said Tori.

"Sorry," Chief said. "That's the Navy life."

Tori folded her arms across her chest. "Well, when I grow up, I'm not going to marry anyone in the Navy or the Army or the Air Force."

"How about the Marines?" I reminded her.

"Or the Marines."

"Don't worry," I told her. "No one will probably want to marry you anyway."

Tori burst into tears and ran out of the kitchen. A second later her bedroom door slammed.

Mom shook her head. "Piper Reed."

"I didn't say she was fat!"

My sister really wasn't fat, even though I sometimes called her that. She was a little chubby though. The last time she got upset, she threatened to go on a hunger strike. She didn't eat for two whole hours.

Mom stood. "I'll check on Tori. Piper, why don't you help clean up?"

"Jeepers! I have to do the dishes just because I'm not a big crybaby? Besides it's Tori's turn."

Chief started stacking plates. "Tell you what, Piper. Show Sam where Pensacola, Florida, is on the map and I'll help your mom."

I saluted him. I was the only daughter who did that, too. My sisters needed to learn some respect. Chief may not be an officer, but he was

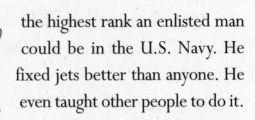

the highest rank an enlisted man could be in the U.S. Navy. He fixed jets better than anyone. He even taught other people to do it.

Sam had a pile of pizza on her plate with the cheese missing. I hated cheese on my pizza, and that's all Sam liked about it.

I took Sam by the hand. "Come on."

Sam and I walked downstairs to Mom's studio. It really wasn't a studio, just a basement where Mom did her art. Mom lighted strawberry-scented candles whenever she worked down there, but I could still smell the fumes from her oil paints.

This was the first home where we lived that wasn't on a military base. When we arrived in San Diego, Mom and Chief found an old gray house to rent with a big yard and a huge climbing tree. A tire swing hung from a low branch. Higher up, Chief had built a tree house. That's where the Gypsy Club met.

I loved the tree house. Chief built it for all of us, but Tori hardly climbed up. And when she did, she never did anything fun. She'd just read a boring book or play Scrabble with one of her boring friends. Sam was only five and too little to climb up there unless Mom, Chief, or Tori went with her. So it was really like the tree house belonged to me.

I'd had a lot of good times in the tree house. I'd lost a front tooth, spied on our neighbors, played pirates with the other Gypsy Club members. Thinking of missing all that stuff made me feel that fish bumping against my belly again.

Sam tugged at my shirt. "Piper, where's Florida?"

Her black curls covered her head like a zillion miniature Slinky toys. No one else in our family had curly hair. Mom said Grandpa Reynolds did when he was younger. But now he didn't have any hair.

Sometimes when Sam was driving me crazy, I liked to pretend she wasn't my real sister. Or sometimes I imagined that I was really the kidnapped daughter of a Gypsy princess. And the kidnappers had gotten scared that they might get caught, so they wrapped me in a blanket and placed me on the doorstep of this family. Of course it was only a dream. Everyone said that Tori and I were the spitting image of Mom with our blond hair.

Sam let out a big sigh and yanked at my shirt sleeve. "Where's Florida?"

"Just a second." She didn't fool me. She knew where Florida was. She just wanted me to point to the wrong state so she could show off.

I touched the part of the map that said San Diego, California. It was kind of hard to read,

but Mom had marked it
with a silver star.

"Here's where
we are now." I
dragged my finger
east, then a little
south. "And here's
Florida."

Florida was easy
to find on the map.
It looked like the
long, skinny bottom
part of a key. I'd
memorized all the
states' shapes for a test we'd had this year. Mon-
tana was shaped like the head of a woman wearing a rectangular hat. Michigan was a mitten
ready to catch a snowball. Nevada looked like a
wide hatchet. I would have gotten a hundred on
that test, if I hadn't misspelled all the words.

"Where's Pepsi-Cola?" Sam asked.

"Pensacola," I corrected her.

"That's what I said—Pepsi-Cola."

I clucked my tongue. "You're just trying to be silly."

Sam was practically a genius. She was already reading chapter books. The principal even gave her special permission to be in the Kick-Off-the-School-Year-Spelling-Bee. When she won, he called her a child prodigy. Tori said a prodigy was someone who could do something better than a lot of people. To me, it meant Sam got her picture in the paper wearing the crown she received as a prize. Sam wanted to wear that crown everywhere, even to church and the mall. It's really embarrassing to walk around with a kid who thinks she's a princess.

Sam yanked on my shirt. "I said, 'Where's Pensacola?' "

"Well, since you pronounced it right, I'll show you."

I had no idea where Pensacola was, so I pointed to a tiny dot in Florida. "Pensacola is right here."

Sam leaned close to the map. "That says Palm Beach."

My face felt hot. "Just seeing if you were paying attention. Find it yourself, Miss Smarty Pants."

Sam took a long moment checking out the Florida part of the map. Then she pressed her tiny finger against a spot. "There it is!"

Gosh, Pensacola was a long way from San Diego. I went over to Mom's desk and flipped through her drawing pad. Mom used to be an art teacher until Sam was born. Now she drew a lot of pictures at home. Inside her drawing pad was a sketch of me and my friends, the other

Gypsy Club members—MacKenzie, Natalie, and Briley. Mom drew it as if she was looking inside the tree house's window.

I turned the page.

"Get off the bus!" I hollered. My Gypsy Club invented that saying. At one meeting, we decided we'd make up a cool phrase that would circle around the whole world. We'd become so famous they'd put our names in the newspaper.

Sam rushed over to me and peered at the tablet. "What?"

"It's Kip! Mom drew Kip and me."

Kip was Mr. Nelson's German shepherd. Mr. Nelson, our next-door neighbor, used to be a policeman and Kip used to be a police dog. When Mr. Nelson retired, Kip retired, too. He was the coolest and smartest dog. He could walk up a slide and slide down. He could play fetch with a Frisbee. He even protected me from the neighborhood bullies when they hung over our fence, calling me names. Whenever they did that, he'd growl and bark. If we ever had a dog, I'd want him to be just like Kip.

"Did Mom draw me?" Sam asked, trying to turn the page.

I shrugged and stared at Mom's sketches— Kip, the tree house, the Gypsy Club. That fish was flipping and flopping. Tori was right. Sometimes being a Navy brat was the pits.

2

SISTER MAGIC

The Gypsy Club came over to say good-bye. So
had Tori's friend Callie. Then, as the packers
loaded the last boxes on the moving truck, Sam
let out one of her famous wails.

"Aaa-nnie! They packed Annie!"

For some reason, a picture of Annie facedown
flashed in my mind.

Mom lowered her shoulders. "Sam, we told
you to put everything on the porch that you
wanted to take in the minivan."

Tori had packed her Scrabble game and her journal where she kept her word collection. She was going to be a poet when she grew up. That's why she got excited over words like *juniper, applesauce,* and *dribble.*

I'd put my color pencils and drawing pad in a pile next to hers. The only thing in Sam's pile was a set of Laura Ingalls Wilder books that her teacher had given her as a going-away present. And, of course, her precious crown was on her head.

The moving men were about to put the mattresses on the truck.

"Are you sure Annie isn't under your bed?" Chief asked.

Annie flashed in my mind again. This time I could see blue fabric hanging above her.

"She's not there," Sam cried. "I already looked. I forgot to put her on the porch. Annie doesn't like to be in dark places by herself."

"Hey," I told her, "maybe Annie wanted to go on an adventure." I would have loved to ride in a huge truck.

Sam folded her arms across her chest. "She doesn't like adventures."

It was true. Annie lived a pretty dull life. Sam couldn't sleep or take a bath without her. That's not a very exciting schedule, even for a doll. I squeezed my eyes shut and tried one more time to see Annie and the blue fabric.

The moving men started to put our blue velvet couch behind the boxes. Then I remembered.

Yesterday, I was chasing a tennis ball that had rolled under the couch. "Annie was under the couch!" I hollered.

Mom hurried over to them. "Wait!" I guess she was thinking about how stinky Sam was going to get if she stopped bathing.

"Is it possible to open a few boxes to look for my daughter's doll?"

The mover pressed his lips together and his face turned chili-pepper red. I thought smoke was going to blow out of his ears.

He wiped the sweat on his forehead with the back of his sleeve. "Ma'am, we just finished with the boxes. We're loading the furniture now."

The other mover, a tall, skinny guy, walked over. "Oh, come on, Kurt. It won't take that long. We labeled the boxes."

"Thank you so much," Mom said.

The skinny guy winked. "Ma'am, I've got a kid who won't go to sleep without his little brown bear."

I stepped toward him. "I think it's in the boxes from the living room."

Sam was still blubbering, and stuff was running out of her nose.

Chief pulled out his handkerchief and squatted next to her. "Here, blow."

The nice man hopped into the truck.

"Hey," Kurt said. "I think I remember throwing it in one of those boxes."

Sam's eyes grew big and she looked as if she was going to cry again. "You threw her?"

Grumpy Kurt ignored her and told the nice guy, "Charlie, it's in one of the living room boxes."

Luckily, those were the last boxes put on the truck, but unluckily, there were eight boxes.

"Hey, little lady," Charlie said to me. "Want to guess which box? You've got us this far."

"Come on, Charlie," Kurt said. "This ain't a game show."

Just then, Mr. Nelson and Kip showed up to say good-bye. Kip wagged his tail when he saw me. Normally I would have run over to pet him, but I was on a mission—a mission to find Annie.

Charlie motioned me onto the ramp that traveled up the back of the truck. My family, the Gypsy Club, Mr. Nelson, and even Kip crowded in close to watch me make my decision. I could

almost hear a drumroll in the background. *Bumpity, bump, bump, bump!* I paced in front of the boxes a couple of times before picking the second to the left. "I think it's in this one."

Red-faced Kurt sighed. Charlie chuckled and asked, "You sure now?"

"Yes, sir."

Charlie dug out his pocketknife and slit through the tape.

I sucked in a big breath as he pulled out Chief's Western books and some knickknacks wrapped in tissue paper. I wanted to be right. He handed the items to Chief, who lined them up on the ground. Finally, Charlie pulled out a doll with half its brown hair missing and a purple marker scribble on her cheek.

"Way to go, Piper!" Mr. Nelson said.

"Get off the bus!" the Gypsy Club yelled.

Kip barked and everyone clapped.

Sam jumped with her arms opened wide.

"Annie! Annie! You saved her!"

Charlie handed the doll to her, and Sam hugged it. "Thank you," she told him.

"Don't thank me," Charlie said. "Thank your sister. I don't think Kurt would have let me open a second box."

Sam hugged me tight, pressing Annie into my ribs.

"Yes, sir," said Charlie. "I guess that's what you call sister magic. That's the kind of magic where you know something just because it's in your genes."

I said good-bye to the Gypsy Club, and Mr. Nelson let me play fetch with Kip one last time. A few minutes later, the moving truck drove away, and soon, so did we. We pulled out of the driveway and on to our street. I wanted to look back, but part of me didn't. Then, just when it was almost too late, I turned and stole a glimpse of the gray house that used to be home.

3

I SPy

Phoenix, Arizona

"**A**re we in Louisiana yet?" Sam asked for about the eighty-millionth time.

"No," Mom said. "We're in Arizona."

Arizona had lots of sand, sky, and cactus. Even the McDonald's had a cactus growing in front of its giant arches. Chief woke us up at the hotel so early that the sky was still dark when we started out on the road. Now the sun peeked above the horizon. It looked like an orange beach ball in the middle of a pink sky.

Mom sighed. "If we lived out here, I'd paint every sunrise."

It was our second day in the minivan. On the way to Florida we'd stop in Louisiana to visit our grandparents. Both Mom's and Chief's parents lived there.

Tori sat in the very back seat, the *best* seat. My parents let us take turns sitting there by ourselves. I couldn't wait until it was my turn. Then I could stretch out, instead of sitting next to Sam and being forced to listen to her read every single billboard. Tori stuffed wadded-up pieces of tissue in her ears so she didn't have to hear her.

Leaning forward, I tried to see the gas needle, but my seat belt held me in place. Chief always filled the gas tank when it was on the quarter mark. That's when it would be my turn to sit in the back.

Sam acted like her reading was a perform-ance. When we passed a Burger King sign, she

dropped her voice and read, "Have it your way."
Then in a squeaky voice—"State Farm is there."

I didn't like to read. Most of the time the words looked jumbled. "Dyslexia," the counselor called it. It sounded like I had some terrible disease and a great way to get out of school assignments.

But when Mom asked "Why didn't you do your report on George Washington?" and I answered "I would have, but I have dyslexia," she looked me straight in the eyes and said, "Don't try to pull that one on me, Piper Reed. I'm dyslexic and I've finished plenty of homework."

A few miles outside of Phoenix, Arizona
Chief exited the highway and pulled in to a convenience store.

There were only two good things about being cooped up in the van with my crazy sisters—snack breaks and McDonald's. Mom teased

Chief that he should have a bumper sticker that read I BRAKE FOR BIG MACS!

"Can we get a snack?" I asked. We'd finished breakfast less than a couple of hours before. But the no-snacks-between-meals rule disappeared on the road.

Somehow, even with the tissue plugged in her ears, Tori heard the word "snack." Her senses had superpowers when it came to food. She unsnapped her seat belt and hopped out of the van quicker than I could say "tornado."

"Wait a minute," Mom said. "Take Sam with you and let her pick out something. And make sure she goes to the bathroom." Sometimes Mom could spoil the fun.

Tori held Sam's hand and I took off ahead of them. Inside, the store smelled like hot dogs and burnt coffee. By the time Tori and Sam reached the bathroom, I'd already picked out a bag of M&M's and an orange soda. Outside, I raced to the very back seat. Ah! The space, the quiet—I could get used to this.

With my seatbelt buckled, I tried different positions. I stretched my legs across the seat. I folded my legs under my bottom. I turned, faced the  back, pointed my toes toward the roof of the van, and let my head hang over the seat.

Rap, rap, rap! All I could see was Sam's  hand waving in front of the open window. "Hey," she yelled. "It's my turn!"

"Since when do *you* get a turn?"

"Mommy and Daddy said I could."

Mom turned around, facing me. "That's right. It's your little sister's turn. You'll be next."

"Jeepers!" I unbuckled and flipped head first over the seat. I was back where I started.

Sam had never wanted to sit in the back seat by herself before. She'd tried on our move to San Diego. Three minutes later she started crying. Chief had to pull over onto the side of a busy interstate and let her get back in the middle row.

"You're not going to cry, are you?" I asked.

"No. I'm a big girl now." Annie was buckled in next to her.

I rolled my eyes. "Ha! Ha! That's so funny I forgot to laugh."

Tori buckled in to the seat next to me. She ate her king-size milk chocolate bar in less than a minute and gulped down her soda. Then she watched me slowly eat my M&M's one by one.

"Mmm, mmm," I said between long sips of my orange drink. "Delicious!"

Tori narrowed her eyes at me. Then she tore off two pieces of tissue, rolled each into a tiny ball, and stuck them in her ears. She flipped open her book, but I knew she was still thinking about my M&M's.

Two days later, Wichita Falls, Texas
"Northwestern Mutual, the quiet company," Sam whispered.

I'd had enough. "Hey, Sam," I said, "want to play a game?"

Sam's eyes grew wide. "What game?"

"The quiet game. Whoever speaks first loses."

Sam smiled. "Okay."

"*Buzz!* You lose!"

Sam poked out her lips. "That's not fair. You didn't say 'start.'"

I sighed. "Okay. Start."

Sam pointed at me. "*Buzz!* You lose!"

How did I get stuck with two goofy sisters?

Chief put on his bluegrass CD, like he did at home sometimes. Sam and I groaned, but then we pinched our noses and joined in. "Keep on the sunny side, always on the sunny side. . . ."

Outside the window, a bunch of cows were in a field next to an old motel called the Yellow Rose. There seemed to be more cows than people in Texas.

We passed a white house with some kids playing in front. I wondered if they'd lived in that house their whole lives. Or did they ever have to move?

Suddenly Sam stopped singing. "Are we in Louisiana yet?"

Mom shook her head. "No. We're just now outside Wichita Falls, Texas."

I wondered how a kid who might be a prodigy couldn't figure out that we weren't in Louisiana.

A little later, we decided to play the "I Spy"

game. Even Mom played. Chief said he had to concentrate on his driving, but we knew he didn't like games. I loved "I Spy" on a road trip because I could see things that no one else did. And how could they prove that I didn't?

"I spy something green," Sam started.

"That car," I said. Sam always picked whatever car was in front of us.

"How did you know?" Sam asked.

I shrugged my shoulders. "Sister magic, I guess."

"Your turn, Piper," Mom said.

I looked around at the passing cars and all the cows. Boring. "I spy something brown."

"A cow!" shouted Sam.

"Warm," I said.

"That truck?" Mom said, excited.

"Cold." What did a truck have to do with a cow?

Tori peeked over her book. I guess those tissue balls didn't always work.

"Dad's hat," Sam guessed.

"Freezing."

Tori put her straw between the pages and closed the book. "Okay. Let's think about this. Piper said 'warm' when Sam said 'cow.' It must have something to do with a cow."

Sam jiggled in her seat. "I know, I know, I know!"

"What?"

"Cow poop!"

"Nope. Give up?"

"No!" Sam and Tori shouted.

"I give up," Mom said.

The ranch dirt, the fence, the tree trunk . . . on and on, they guessed. Finally, Tori said, "I give up! It's probably something dumb anyway."

Sam lowered her eyebrows and frowned. "I won't give up. I'm putting my thinking cap on."

She dug the crown out of her backpack and placed it on her head.

"Give up, Sam," said Tori. "Then it will be your turn."

"It won't be your turn if you give up," I reminded them.

"Okay, so you get to go again," Tori said. "Big deal."

"All right." Sam folded her arms across her chest. "I give up."

I took a breath, then announced, "A two-headed cow."

"What?" Tori shouted.

Sam stretched her neck toward the window. "Where? Where's the two-headed cow?"

"Oh, we already passed it down the road."

Mom giggled, but I could tell she was trying not to. Chief glanced from the odometer to the road. I don't think he heard a word we said.

"That's not fair, Piper," Tori said.

Now Sam was crying. "I wanted to see the two-headed cow. You could have pointed to it before I missed it."

"THERE IS NO TWO-HEADED COW!" yelled Tori. "SHE MADE IT UP!"

"That's enough, girls!" Chief ordered.

"Yes, sir," I said, saluting.

Arlington, Texas

We spent the night at a hotel in Arlington. From our window we had a great view of a roller coaster at the Six Flags amusement park.

"Can we go tomorrow?" I asked.

"Sorry," Chief said. "We have to stay on schedule. If we don't leave by o-eight hundred, we'll arrive after dark."

My heart sank. A few rides on the roller coaster would be worth missing a few hours with our relatives. I hadn't been on a roller coaster

yet, and it was definitely on my list of things I had
to do before fifth grade.

The next morning, Chief gassed up the van
before leaving the city. At least it was my turn for
the back seat. That made up for not getting to go
to Six Flags. Well, almost. We drove by the park
gate, where hundreds of people were lining up.

"See?" Chief said. "Just think of all those long lines we're going to miss."

Tori sank lower in her seat. "I heard they sell funnel cakes there."

Marshall, Texas

A few hours later, tall pine trees lined the road and the air turned sticky. East Texas looked a lot like the part of Louisiana where my grandparents lived.

"Are we in Louisiana now?" Sam asked.

"No," I said. "We're still in Texas."

"But this doesn't look like that other Texas."

"Texas is big," Mom told her.

"Texas used to be a whole other country," Chief said.

"It still is," joked Mom.

"Johnny B. Goode" played out from the radio. That was Chief's favorite song. He sang along with the guy on the radio and tapped the dash-board with his right hand. Mom passed around her hairbrush, and we took turns pretending it was a microphone. At the end of the song, we all yelled "Johnny B. Goode!"

After the song finished, Mom flicked off the

radio. "Hey, y'all, why don't we sing our favorite songs?"

That's what happens when you get cooped up inside a car with your family for days and days. Even something dumb like singing songs into a hairbrush seems fun.

We sang "Country Roads." Only instead of singing "West Virginia," we filled in "Lou-i-si-ana." Then right smack in the middle of that song, the highway turned from smooth to bumpy, and we passed a sign that read WELCOME TO LOUISIANA. It happened so fast it was like a blur.

Sam stopped singing and turned around, staring at the back of the sign. "Are we in Louisiana?"

Everyone shouted, "Yes!"

4

ADVENTURES iN PiNEY WOODS

PINEY WOODS, POPULATION 492. Sam read the sign as we drove through the small town where Mom and Chief grew up. We passed the post office, Miss Vicki's Vittles, a Laundromat, and a little store.

After we drove by Mom and Chief's old school, we entered the woods where Grandma and Grandpa Reed lived. The longleaf pines grew tall and thick along the winding road.

Chief rolled down his window, and a pine scent drifted into the van.

Mom's shoulders rose as she took a long whiff. "We're home," she said. Her voice sounded all crackly.

Chief stretched his arm across the seat and touched her shoulder. "Yep, we're home."

A moment later we pulled onto my grandparents' gravel driveway. Our relatives poured out of the house to greet us. There were grandparents, uncles, aunts, and cousins. We hadn't seen them for two years. Everyone must have missed us something awful because the grownups attacked us with lots of hugs and kisses.

"My goodness," Aunt Lynette said, smoothing down my hair. "Sam, you've grown taller than a bean stalk since I last laid eyes on you."

"I'm not Sam. I'm Piper."

"Gracious, child. Don't mess with my head." Then she went over to Sam and stared at her like

she'd never seen her before. "Edie, I didn't know
you'd gone off and had another child. Where'd
you get that crown, little princess?"

Sam puffed out her chest. "I got it from being
a prodigy."

"Oh," said Aunt Lynette.

Mom placed her hands on Sam's shoulders. "Not exactly. Her school gave it to her when she won the spelling bee."

Uncle Riley winked at me. "Are you still that champion Scrabble player?"

"That's not me," I said. "That's Tori."

He poked his elbow in my ribs. "Oh, come on now, you don't have to be bashful with your old Uncle Riley."

My cousins, Megan and Collin, stood by watching while we got squeezed like tubes of toothpaste. They probably were used to it because they lived in a house down the road. I wondered what it would be like to live near my grandparents all year long.

"Guess what?" Collin said. "We get to sleep on the screen porch."

That night, Tori and I dressed in our blue pajamas Mom bought for the trip. Then we rolled out our sleeping bags on the screen porch with Megan and Collin.

The stars became glitter sprinkled across black velvet. For a while, I watched fireflies dance around the trees. I was about to fall asleep when Megan cupped her hand over Tori's ear and whispered some silly secret. Then they giggled.

I recited the words that Tori had taught me. "Secrets, secrets are no fun, unless you're telling everyone."

They ignored me, though, and kept giggling.

So I said, "Pssst, Collin?"

Collin raised his eyelids. "Yeah?"

"Remember the last time I was here?"

He rubbed his eyes. "No. That was a long time ago."

"You know," I said. "Ten little monkeys jumping on the bed?"

"Oh, yeah," Collin whispered. "I remember."

Then we stood and began jumping and singing, "Ten little monkeys jumping on the bed . . ."

We jumped and jumped, and sang and sang.

When we did that a few years ago, it drove Tori and Megan crazy, but now they ignored us. We got louder.

"Nine little monkeys jumping on the bed. One fell off and—"

"Stop it right now!" Megan snapped. "Or else!"

"—bumped his head," I yelled, but Collin didn't say a word. He stopped jumping and lay back down. His eyes were tightly shut.

I gave him a gentle nudge. "Come on."

Collin shook his head, not bothering to open his eyes. "Uh-uh. Have you ever felt Megan's punch before?"

Then his head disappeared into the sleeping bag like a scared turtle tucking into its shell.

Tori could scream louder than anyone I knew.

Once she even pulled my hair, but at least she didn't sock me. I fell asleep, dreaming about Megan using poor Collin as a punching bag.

The next morning, Grandpa Reed and Uncle Seth saddled up Buster, the Shetland pony. All of us older cousins took turns riding him.

"Do you know how to ride horseback?" Megan asked me while I waited for my turn.

"Of course," I said. "I rode the last time I was here." Then I spat on the ground like a tough cowgirl.

"Gross!" Megan and Tori sang together.

When Collin returned with Buster, it was my turn. I put my right foot in the stirrup, swung my left leg over, and settled into the saddle.

Everyone burst into laughter, pointing at me. I stared straight ahead. Buster's tail swept side to side. His head seemed to have disappeared.

Collin laughed the loudest.
"Piper got on Buster back-
wards!"

Megan smirked. "Thought
you said you knew how to
ride?"

I sat up tall. "I like riding this way."

"Yeah, sure," Megan
said.

I ignored her, but see-
ing Tori laugh made me
want to disappear.

Uncle Seth helped me off.
Then he lifted the left stirrup. "Try this one
first."

This time, I slid my left foot into the stirrup
and swung my right leg over. Now Buster's head
was where it should be. I was ready to ride. But
before I could grab the reins, a bee buzzed near

my face and I tried to swat it away. Then the bee flew toward Buster's ear, and since Buster couldn't swat, he took off running instead.

My breath left me and I felt as if I was racing after it. I seized the saddle horn and bent low, dodging the branches. Buster kept running, weaving in between the tall trunks.

Everyone sprinted after us.

"Grab the reins!" Megan yelled.

"Hold on tight!" Grandpa Reed hollered.

"Watch out for the branches!" Tori called out.

"You're doing fine!" said Uncle Seth. "Hang on, now!"

"Lean forward!" Collin shouted.

"Don't fall, Piper!" cried Sam.

I was afraid Buster would keep running if everyone kept chasing us. My heart thumped against my chest. I closed my eyes. I yelled, but my words came out quivery. "St-stop! St-stop!"

Suddenly Buster broke into a smooth gallop.

It felt like I was in a Western movie. I opened my eyes and stretched one arm toward the sky. "Yee-haw!"

But then I noticed we were heading toward the barbed-wire fence. I muttered, "Help, help, help, help, help, help." I leaned way to the right and the saddle slid to the side with my feet stuck in the stirrups. My fingers gripped the saddle horn tighter. I must have looked like a trick rodeo rider.

A few feet from the fence, Buster slowed his pace and then stopped.

The saddle slid more until I hung upside down, dangling under Buster's belly. Grass became sky. Sky became grass. A pair of cowboy boots and tennis shoes hurried toward me.

"Is it time to swim?" I asked.

Swimming at Rambling Creek went a lot smoother. The water was icy cold, but after I dunked my whole body, it felt refreshing. We played water tag until our fingers pruned. Then we dried off, hurried back to the house, and changed into dry clothes.

Thank goodness, it was time to eat, because swimming made me hungry.

The adults ate at the kitchen table. All the cousins ate out on the screen porch.

"This is delicious," Megan said through a big mouthful of french fries.

For a long time, no one said anything. We just ate.

Sometimes when it was too quiet, words floated into my head and before I knew it they'd popped out of my mouth. "I'm a vegetarian," I announced.

Collin pointed to my hamburger. "What's that then?"

"Except for hamburgers," I said.

"How about pizza?" Tori asked. "You mean you're never gonna eat pepperoni pizza again?"

"Well, I'm a vegetarian, except for hamburgers and pepperoni pizza."

Megan rolled her eyes. "You're weird, Piper."

Tori giggled. "Yeah, Piper Weirdo."

What was happening to Tori? Hanging around Megan was turning her into a meanie.

Sam asked, "What's a weirdo?"

"Go look it up in the dictionary," Megan said.

"You'll find a picture of Piper right next to the word."

The only thing tougher than being a middle child was being a middle child who was also a vegetarian.

If you love being squished and squeezed and kissed to death, then you would enjoy a Piney Woods good-bye.

The morning we set out for Florida, I felt like

a piece of Play-Doh being forced through a plastic what-cha-ma-jigger that turns Play-Doh into shapes. But by the time I made it to the end of the send-off line, I hadn't turned into a cool star or a long, skinny tube. I'd just changed into a mussed-up version of me.

Pink and red lipstick kisses polka-dotted my face. My hair was tousled and my clothes looked wrinkly. After smelling the aunts' and grandmas' floral perfumes, I needed lots of fresh oxygen.

When we got into the van, the relatives were still waving and saying good-bye. And our grandmas even poked their heads inside the open windows for more kisses.

Grandpa Reed knocked on Sam's door. "See you later, alligator."

Sam sang back, "In a while, crocodile!"

Chief started the engine and hollered, "Don't be a stranger! Pensacola isn't that far."

I stuck my head out the window and yelled,

"Yeah, come visit, but leave that mean ole Megan at home!"

Suddenly a fist hit my arm. "Ouch!" I yelled, glaring at Tori. "You never punched me before."

"There's a first time for everything."

5

A NEW HOME

The empty townhouse smelled like fresh paint. And our words bounced off the bare walls.

"I have to share a room with Sam?" My old bedroom was twice this size, and I didn't have to share with anybody.

Mom frowned. "Well, someone has to share a room. There are only three bedrooms. It's only fair that Tori has her own room. She's the—"

"Oldest!" I said. "Why isn't there ever anything special for the middle child?"

Chief cleared his throat. "That's enough, Piper."

"I don't mind sharing a room," Sam said.

"Of course not," I said. "You're a scaredy-cat. You usually end up in Mom and Chief's bed anyway."

"Do not!"

"Do so!"

"Okay," said Chief. "The next person who speaks gets last place in the bathroom order." Then he added, "Permanently."

There was only one bathroom in the townhouse. Chief had already posted a list with bathroom orders plainly written out. Each day, the last person on the list rotated to the top. That way, every Reed had a turn to be first.

I'd started a list, too. My Why-I-Wish-We'd-Never-Moved list.

1. I had my own room in San Diego.
2. We had two bathrooms in our old house.

"Why can't we live in one of those big houses with the screen porches?" I asked.

"That's the officers' housing," Chief said. "These homes are for enlisted families."

Mom's arm surrounded my shoulders and pulled me closer. "This is a nice home, Piper. Hey, where's that Gypsy spirit?"

I shrugged, but I wanted to say, *It's back in my tree house in San Diego.*

3. I had a tree house in San Diego.

I looked out the window at the backyard. This yard didn't even have a tree. It was almost too small for a swing set. What would keep Sam from pestering me?

Chief grabbed his keys. "Your mom and I need to get groceries from the commissary. Why don't y'all come along for the ride? We'll tour the base so you can see everything. We'll even drive by the beach."

"Can we go by my school?" Sam asked.

"You bet. The schools are off-base, so we'll check them out after we go to the commissary. Cheer up, girls. Besides, your mom and I have a surprise after dinner."

"Ice cream?" Sam asked.

"No. We have an announcement."

"What?" I asked.

"After dinner," Chief said.

I hated waiting for surprises. Every Christmas morning I woke up before the whole family just to see what everybody got before they did.

"Can't you tell us now?" Sam begged.

Chief winked. "You'll have to wait."

Walking to the van, Tori whispered to me. "I hope they're not having a baby."

"Why do you think that?" I asked.

"The last time they made a surprise announcement they told us we were moving here. So it's not that. The only other announcement they ever made was when they were expecting Sam. You don't remember because you were too little."

"I do, too, remember." But I was lying. I knew why Tori didn't want another sister or a brother though—so she wouldn't have to share her room with anyone.

* * *

We drove around the base. It was a pretty base, as far as bases go. Palm trees and flowers grew in front of the chapel and the hospital. From the road, we could see the Gulf. The recreation area had a pool and some tennis courts.

Chief pointed to the movie theater. "Maybe we can go see a movie before I leave for ship duty."

"Before you leave?" I asked.

"I leave in two weeks."

I'd been so busy thinking of how my life was going to change in Florida, I'd forgotten about Chief leaving. A lump blocked my throat. I glanced over at Tori. Her cheek was pressed against the window. I wondered if she was already missing Chief like I was. How could you miss somebody who hadn't even left yet?

"Will we get to have our special dinners?" Sam asked.

"You bet," said Chief.

The week before he shipped out, we each got to go to dinner alone with him one night. Mom got two dinners alone because Chief said she was extra special. We also got to pick anyplace we wanted to go before dinner, as long as it wasn't someplace like the Eiffel Tower or Disney World.

We drove by the beach on the base. Jet Skis and boats bounced on the waves.

"The beach is close to our new house!" I yelled. I bet I could walk to the beach all by myself.

Then, as if he read my mind, Chief said, "You

girls don't go to the beach without your mom."

We passed the Naval Aviation Museum. At the entrance, a gray jet pointed toward the sky.

"Get off the bus!" I said.

"What happens if you get *on* the bus?" Tori asked.

"I guess you go somewhere," I told her.

"Hmmph." Tori shook her head.

Just past the museum, Chief pointed to a blue jet and some airplane hangars. "There's where the Blue Angels work."

"Blue Angels?" I asked. "That's a weird name."

Tori straightened. "I've seen the Blue Angels."

"You sure have," said Chief. "And so have you, Piper. Only you probably don't remember. You were too young."

Why is it that everything exciting seemed to have happened when I was too young and now I couldn't remember any of it?

Chief glanced at me in the rearview mirror. "It was when we were stationed in Corpus Christi. You were a baby."

I was born in Corpus Christi, but, of course, I was too young and now I don't remember it.

"Have I seen the Blue Angels?" Sam asked.

"No, but you will," Chief said. "When they're home, they practice on Tuesday and Wednesday mornings. The Blue Angels are a team of Navy pilots."

"And Marines," Mom added. Her uncle was a Marine, and she never let Chief forget it.

Chief smiled. "Yep, and Marine pilots, too. As I was saying, they're some of the top pilots in the service. They don't just fly."

"They do flips and tricks in the air," Tori said, then added, "I remember."

Chief gave her a thumbs-up. "That's right. Pensacola is the home of the Blue Angels."

"Can we go see them practice?" I asked.

"You'll be able to see them practice from our backyard."

I opened my mouth. "Get—"

"OFF THE BUS!" shouted Tori and Sam.

We drove a few miles away to a nearby base that had the larger commissary. While Mom and Chief shopped for groceries, we drank soft drinks and ate french fries at the McDonald's next door.

Tori wrote in her notebook while Sam

read *The Long Winter*. As I chewed on a salty french fry, I noticed a man walking by with his German shepherd. I added to my list:

4. Kip isn't here.

Then a group of kids my age showed up.

5. The Gypsy Club isn't here.

Twenty minutes later, Mom and Chief walked out of the commissary with two grocery carts filled with brown sacks.

"Wow!" Sam said. "Are we having a party?"

Mom laughed. "It takes a lot of food when you're starting from scratch. We bought a frozen pizza for tonight."

"Yum!" Tori said.

"Pepperoni?" I asked.

"Of course," Mom said. "Is there any other kind?"

Tori smirked. "Yeah, we wouldn't want the vegetarian to have to eat Italian sausage."

Chief loaded the sacks in the back. The

van soon smelled like apples, pears, and onions.

After Chief finished, he got behind the wheel and headed off-base. Mom studied the map he handed her, trying to find the street where the school was.

She turned the map upside down, then sideways. Then she sighed and folded it. "I can never figure out what's north or south."

Finally she handed the map to Tori, who was an expert at north, south, east, *and* west.

Tori told Dad where to turn, and a few minutes later we reached the Blue Angels Elementary School.

Maybe the Blue Angels would visit our school and ask for volunteers to fly in their jets with them. I'd probably be the only student to raise a hand—everyone else would be afraid. Of course, they would pick me. We'd fly way up above the clouds and do a flip. Then the pilot would spell my name with jet smoke across

PIPER

the sky. And I'd wave at all my classmates below.

Chief turned out of the parking lot. "Well, you'll see more of your school Tuesday when we take you."

"Do they have a kindergarten class there?" Sam asked.

"You bet," Chief said.

Sam lit up like a Christmas tree. She was probably looking forward to showing off what a great reader she was in front of a whole new audience.

"You better not wear your crown," I told her. "You'll get teased if you do."

The last time I got teased was before I was tested and I'd had to read in front of the entire class. I wondered if my new teacher would know that I had dyslexia. After I got tested, I had a special teacher who helped me with reading in a tiny room next to the library. I didn't have to read in front of anyone except her.

What if my new teacher made me though? And what if the kids laughed? My throat felt like I had a bunch of cotton balls stuffed inside it.

Then I had a brilliant idea. I'd just say I might need glasses. I felt better already and I stared up at the sky, hoping a Blue Angel would fly by.

When we left my school, we drove by Tori's

middle school. Then we headed back to the base. A few minutes later, we passed the gate guard, who motioned Chief onto the base. As we drove through, I thought about saluting him, but I got in trouble for doing that a long time ago when I was little. I *do* remember that.

Our furniture wouldn't arrive until tomorrow, so we ate on top of a blanket Mom had spread out on the living room floor. It was fun having a picnic indoors. Especially since we didn't have to worry about the ants.

After dinner, Chief said, "Here are your chore lists."

In a spooky voice, Mom said, "The list monster strikes again."

Chief rolled his eyes but handed out the lists anyway. Even Sam got one this time. She acted like it was really something big and started marching around the room, reading hers aloud.

"Sam's Chores. 1. Make your bed before

breakfast. 2. Wipe off the table after each meal. 3. Dust the coffee table twice a week. 4.——"

"Was this the surprise announcement?" I asked, looking down at my chores.

"The lists?" Chief chuckled. "No. The surprise is something your mother and I have been discussing for a while now. We've decided this is the perfect time."

"Oh no," Tori muttered. "I knew it."

Tori better not get too comfortable staying in that room by herself.

We waited for them to say something. Chief wrapped his arm around Mom. "Your mother and I have decided we're going to let you have a dog."

6

My Dream Come True
(Sort of)

My heart was a Ping-Pong ball, bouncing against my chest. I pictured myself walking a German shepherd, *my* German shepherd. I would teach him tricks just like Kip knew. Better than Kip. By the time I was done training him, he'd put Kip to shame. Then I felt a little guilty. I loved Kip. There was no reason to top him. If our German shepherd could be as good as Kip, that would be good enough for me.

"A dog!" Sam squealed. "Oh, a cute little puppy!"

"Not little," I said. "German shepherds are big puppies."

"German shepherd?" Tori rolled her eyes. "No way."

Sam looked as if she was about to burst into tears. "I don't like German shepherds."

She was always afraid of Kip. His loud barks sounded scary, but he'd never hurt her. Every time the neighborhood meanies came around, he ran along the fence and barked. It was a tall fence, but those guys walked on the other side of the street after that.

"Sorry, Piper," Mom said. "A German shepherd is too big."

"No, it's not."

"Piper, listen to your mother," Chief said, pointing toward the window. "Look at the size of our yard. It would be cruel to get a dog as big as Kip."

"Every single day, I'd walk him. I promise. He can even share my bed."

"Mom," Tori said, "make her stop."

"A German shepherd is too big," Mom repeated, this time more firmly.

"How about a little German shepherd?" I asked.

Chief laughed. "There is no such thing as a *little* German shepherd."

"How about a poodle?" Tori asked. "They're smart, cute, and *little*."

"Aunt Sophie has a poodle," Mom said. "It won all kinds of ribbons at dog shows."

I'd seen those ribbons when we visited Aunt Sophie a few years ago. They covered an entire wall in her den. She had pictures of Fee Fee or Foo Foo or whatever its name was all over the house. Now it was just a fat dog that liked to sniff crotches.

Sam bounced in her chair. "I want a poodle, too. A fluffy one."

"A poodle?" I wrinkled my nose. Finally we had a chance to get a dog and my sisters wanted a prissy poodle.

Mom smiled. "A poodle is a terrific choice."

"Yay!" yelled my sisters. Tori grabbed Sam and

danced her around the room. "We win! We get a poodle!"

I sank lower in the couch.

Mom settled next to me and put her arm around my shoulders. "Tell you what, Piper. Since your sisters chose the breed of dog, you can name it."

I sprang to my feet. "Get off the bus!"

That night in bed, I could hear Tori reading her poetry through the vent between our rooms.

"No one hears the sound of sand. Everyone hears the ocean crashing on the shore. But would the ocean make a sound without the sand?"

I thought about answering, "Who cares?" But then I realized the vent would be a great way to spy on Tori. If only she'd say something interesting.

In the other bed, Sam hugged Annie close to her and said, "Don't worry, Annie. I'll always love you even though we're getting a cute little puppy."

All night long in bed I thought of names. Kip? No, there was just one Kip. Spot? Max? I decided I'd just wait until I met him. Then I'd pick a name that fit.

Chief bought a newspaper the next morning, and at breakfast he searched the PETS FOR SALE column in the classified section. He took a swig of coffee, then swallowed. "Oh, here we go. 'Adorable peach-colored poodle puppies. Only three remaining. Two males and one female. No papers.'"

Adorable? Yuck. Peach? Phooey. Poodle? Lousy.

Chief dialed the phone number to get directions. After Tori and I washed the breakfast dishes, our family headed out in the van to the poodle lady's house.

On the way, Sam sang, "How much is that doggie in the window?"

"Ruff, ruff!" barked Chief.

Mom and Tori giggled because Chief hardly ever acted silly. It's probably against the Navy rules.

While they sang and laughed, I thought of names. None of them seemed to fit an adorable peach poodle. I could only think of German shepherd names—Rufus, King, Rin Tin Tin.

Sam stretched on her tip-toes at the lady's house and rang the doorbell. It played "Yankee Doodle."

Finally, the door opened. The poodle lady wore a pink terry-cloth bathrobe, and her silver hair was rolled up in hot curlers. She looked like she'd used a blue crayon on her eyebrows. If it were Halloween, she'd scare a few kids away before they could say "Trick or Treat."

"Sorry for my appearance," she said in a gravelly voice. "It's been a busy morning since I talked to you on the phone. In fact, we only have one puppy left. Hope you want a female."

"Why not?" Chief said. "Our house is already filled with them."

A female? Jeepers, I thought. She'd probably be extra prissy.

The lady's house smelled like she had a whole bunch of dogs. Newspaper with big wet spots covered the floor. I'll bet German shepherds don't stink. We stepped carefully past the kitchen, where a grown poodle watched us from behind a short gate. She wagged her pom-pom tail.

The lady disappeared down a hallway, then returned with a peach-colored puppy. It looked like a stuffed toy. It had a miniature tail with a tiny pom-pom on the end.

"Oh, she's so cute," Sam squeaked. "Can I hold her?"

"Be careful," the lady said, giving the puppy over to my little sister. "She's just a baby."

Sam gently held the puppy.

I hated to admit it, but that puppy was cute.

"She's perfect," Tori said.

The puppy whimpered. Forget dog tricks. I was probably going to have to teach this dog to bark. Or maybe the puppy was just scared to death of my sisters' giant faces coming at her and all their goo-goo, ga-ga sounds.

"She's a miniature," the poodle lady said. "Not as tiny as a toy breed, but she'll be small when she's grown."

"That's great," Mom said. "She'll be a good lapdog."

Kip would never want to sit on anyone's lap.

Chief paid the poodle lady, and we left, with Sam carrying the puppy all the way to the car.

Inside the car, Sam said, "I think her name should be Peaches."

Tori tried it out. "Peaches. That's a cute name. I like it."

"Hey," I reminded them, "I get to name the dog, remember?"

"That's right," Chief said. "Tori, you and Sam picked the breed. Piper gets to choose the name."

Tori stared at me. "Well? What's it going to be?"

"Bruno," I said.

"Bruno?" Tori snapped. "No way!"

"That's not a good name," Sam cried.

"Well, it's not a good name for a person," I said. "But it's a great name for a dog."

"She needs a girl's name," Sam said.

"Piper," Mom said softly, "Bruno might cause some confusion at the vet's office. Can't you think of something a little more feminine?"

"Okay," I said. "Bruna."

"Mom!" Tori whined.

"Well . . ." Mom started.

"You said I could pick the name. I want *Bruna*."

"Uh-oh!" Sam said. "Bruna just wee-weed on me."

It looked like there was a lot I was going to have to teach that dog.

7

MORNING ROUTINE

Tuesday morning, Chief flicked the overhead light eight times. "Rise and shine, troops! It's o-seven hundred. You need to be ready to leave by o-eight hundred."

I pulled the blanket over my head. I'd never dreaded the first day of school until today. That's because it wasn't everyone's first day—just ours. And I was still sleepy. I'd stayed up late under the covers with a flashlight, making invitations for the new Gypsy Club.

Gypsy Club was hard to spell. So I drew a Gypsy on each invitation instead. I used purple, yellow, blue, and orange crayons for their clothes. Maybe the invitations would help me make new friends.

Bruna had tinkled on me—again—and my damp nightgown clung to my stomach. She was supposed to sleep in the little cage Mom called a kennel. Bruna didn't like it much though. Her first night at our house, I heard her whining in Tori's room. Tori and Sam slept through thunderstorms and earthquakes. Not me. I woke up if I heard an ant crawl across the floor.

That night, I rescued Bruna and let her sleep with me. I placed her at the foot of my bed, but she moved up my legs and tummy until she reached my neck. Soon, I felt her smooth tongue licking my chin.

Shortly after Chief turned on the light, I slid the covers down below my nose and peeked across the room. Sam's bed was empty. She

probably couldn't wait for school. In other words, she probably couldn't wait to show off.

Chief appeared in the doorway again. "Piper, you're going to be late for mess hall." Mess hall was what the Navy called the place where they ate their meals, but Chief called our kitchen that, too.

The bed creaked as I rolled off my mattress. I took Bruna outside to see if she'd do her business, but she kept jumping on me, wanting to play. Finally I figured she didn't need to do her business. She'd already done it on me. I gave up and we went inside.

I needed to get out of my stinky nightgown and take a shower. But it was too late. Tori was already in the bathroom. That could take forever.

Sam hurried with Annie toward the bathroom door, wearing her stupid crown. "I'm next!" she hollered.

"You forgot about the list," I reminded her. "You're last."

Sam rubbed her eyes. "But I have to go *real bad*."

"Okay. *Real quick* because I get to shower next." I pounded on the door. "THAT'S IF TORI REED EVER DECIDES TO GET OUT OF THE BATH-ROOM!"

"LEAVE ME ALONE!" Tori shouted back.

I was feeling grumpier by the minute. "Sam, you're not going to wear your crown to school, are you?"

Sam frowned. "Why not?"

"I told you. You'll get teased. No one likes a show-off."

"Piper," Mom called from the kitchen, "you and Sam come eat breakfast. I made pancakes."

Sam crossed her legs and bounced. "I can't eat when I have to go to the bathroom."

Mom came down the hall. Splashes of pancake batter decorated her pajama top. She tapped on the bathroom door. "Tori, your little sister needs to go. It's kind of an emergency. Can't you finish getting ready in your room?"

"Just a second," Tori said.

The knob turned, and the door slowly opened. Tori stepped out wearing her kimono. Chief bought kimonos for Tori and me when he was in Japan a couple of years ago.

Tori inched toward her room, making a *swish-swish* sound as she moved.

Sam rushed into the bathroom and slammed the door. I leaned against the wall and waited. Again.

Sam began to sing. "Row, row, row your boat . . ."

"Sam, hurry!"

"That's the only way I can go."

"I thought you said you had to go real bad."

"I did, but now I don't." Then she started again. "Row, row, row your boat . . ."

Mom used to sing that song to help us go potty when we were little.

Sam finally came out, holding a lotion bottle. "What's Thinner Thigh Lotion for?"

"Guess somebody wants to have thinner thighs," I said. I grabbed the bottle from her and hurried inside the bathroom.

Soon, Tori was knocking on the bathroom door and frantically turning the knob. "Let me in. I left something in there."

"What?" I asked, staring at the lotion. "I'll give it to you. Just tell me what you want."

"You know what."

"No, I don't. Unless you mean this?" I cracked the door open and showed her the Thinner Thigh Lotion.

Tori snatched the bottle from my hand. That's when I saw a flash of her leg covered in plastic wrap.

I pointed at her thigh. "You look like a sandwich."

Tori's face turned sunburn red in one second flat. "You're mean, Piper Reed. You're not going to make any friends at your new school."

I felt like she put a curse on me. And later, when we got to school, I thought she had.

8

NEW

An hour after Tori's curse, I stood in my new shoes, next to my new teacher, at the front of my new classroom.

"Boys and girls," Ms. Gordon said, "I'd like to present our new student, Piper Reed."

I'd never been presented before. Ms. Gordon made it sound like I was covered in wrapping paper with a huge bow on top of my head. Strange faces looked my way and stared at me.

My shoes pinched my toes. I tucked my hands

in my pockets and felt my Gypsy Club invitations for good luck. Today I planned to sit at the back of the class and search for my new friends. Then I'd give each of them an invitation. It would be kind of like going to a candy counter, only instead of choosing between M&M's, Reese's Peanut Butter Cups, or sour jawbreakers, I'd select which lucky kids would get to be members of the Gypsy Club.

"Piper," Ms. Gordon said, "how about sitting at this empty desk?" She pointed at a desk on the front row.

"No, thank you."

"Excuse me?" Ms. Gordon peered over her big, round glasses.

"No, thank you, Ms. Gordon."

"I'm sorry, Piper, but I don't think I gave you a choice."

"Yes, you did."

"Pardon?"

"You said, 'How about sitting at this empty desk?'"

A girl on the front
row nodded and
said, "Yes, Ms.
Gordon. You sure
did. You said—"

"I know what
I said." Ms. Gor-
don sounded like
Mom did when
she ordered me
to clean my room.

The girl smiled real big at me. She had braces
with orange and black rubber bands. I'd be cer-
tain to give her a Gypsy Club invitation.

Ms. Gordon took a deep breath and said in
a softer voice, "I shouldn't have asked, Piper,
because this is where you are going to sit."

I didn't like sitting on the front row. How

could I scope out the class for new friends? How could I pass out Gypsy Club invitations, sitting a few feet away from Ms. Gordon's eagle eyes? I couldn't daydream on the front row. I'd have to sit up straight and act like I was paying attention the whole time. On the front row, all I could get was a good look at the blackboard.

At least I was sitting next to the girl with the braces. I studied the boy to my left. He turned toward me, crossed his eyes, and stuck his tongue way out, then licked his nose.

"How'd you do that?" I whispered.

He scowled as if he couldn't believe I'd ask something so stupid.

"Well?" I asked louder. "How'd you do it?"

Ms. Gordon cleared her throat. "Piper, you can meet your new friends at recess time, okay?"

"When's that?" I asked.

"When's what?" she asked.

"Recess."

Ms. Gordon's eyelid began to twitch. Then she said, "Umm, ten o'clock. But right now we're learning about fractions."

She turned, and when she wrote a fraction, the chalk screeched against the blackboard. I winced and covered my ears. So did the kids next to me.

Every time she faced the board, I stole a glimpse at the clock. Eight thirty. A couple of minutes later I checked again. Eight thirty-two. Ten o'clock was going to take forever getting here.

Finally, the bell rang. All the kids took off like a fire alarm had sounded. The girl with the braces stood at my desk. "My name is Nicole. Want to go to recess with me?"

"Okay," I said, following her to the playground.

The other kids played handball, hopscotch, or tag. Nicole leaned against the wall and smiled. Her braces reflected the sun and I had to turn away. She sure smiled a lot.

"What do you do at recess?" I asked.

"This is it."

"This?" Jeepers. I'd made my first friend at my new school, and she didn't do anything at recess except act like a grinning statue.

"I can't play too hard," she explained. "I have a weak stomach."

Then I remembered my Gypsy Club invitations. "Want to join my Gypsy Club?" I wasn't sure I wanted to waste an invitation on her, but after all, she was my first official friend at my new school.

"Sure," Nicole said. "What do you do?"

If this had been San Diego, I could have said, Hang out in my tree house and keep my little sister Sam away. But now I didn't know how to answer that. "Umm . . . we do all kinds of things."

"Do you tell fortunes?"

"Sure." We'd never done that in San Diego.

"Do you tell them, or does a real Gypsy tell them?"

In my entire life, I'd never met a real Gypsy. But my future in Pensacola might depend on that answer. I crossed my fingers behind my back and said, "A real Gypsy, of course."

"Can I invite my brother, too?"

"How old is your brother? This isn't a little kids' club."

"He's not little. He's in our class."

"How can your brother be in our class?"

"That's him." She pointed across the playground to a boy playing handball. He was the boy who could lick his nose and cross his eyes at the same time.

"Get off the bus!"

Nicole glanced around. "What bus?"

"That's your brother?"

"Uh-huh. That's Michael. He's my twin. He has straight teeth."

Now there was someone I could be friends with!

A roar above caused me to look at the sky. A jet was spiraling down. "Oh no!" I yelled.

Nicole giggled. "It's one of the Blue Angels. They're practicing."

The jet straightened and zoomed off. My gaze followed the smoke until it evaporated. Then two jets appeared, flying close together. Suddenly, leaning against the wall and watching didn't seem too bad.

After recess, Ms. Gordon announced, "Time for reading, class."

My head pounded as I watched kids take out their books.

The door opened and a pretty lady walked into our room. She looked too young to be a mom or a teacher.

"Piper," Ms. Gordon said, motioning me over to her desk.

My heart beat faster the closer I got to Ms. Gordon. Did I do something wrong? Was she going to make me stand in front of everyone and read?

"Piper, this is Ms. Mitchell. She's going to be your reading teacher."

My eyes scanned the room to see if any of the kids heard, but only Michael was looking our way. My stomach felt queasy.

Ms. Mitchell held out her hand. "Hi, Piper. What a pleasure."

I took hold of her hand and shook it. I smiled. Ms. Mitchell thought I was a pleasure. My stomach felt better already.

"Let's go down the hall to my room," she said.

I followed Ms. Mitchell to her classroom. The entire way, three words played over and over in my mind. *I'm a pleasure. I'm a pleasure.*

By the end of the day I'd given all four Gypsy Club cards away—to Nicole and Michael, then one to a girl named Kami who gave me two quarters so I could buy ice cream at lunch, and the last one to Hailey, a redheaded girl who had gotten in trouble for talking during social studies.

Now all I needed to do was find a real Gypsy fortune-teller.

After school, I waited in front for Sam. A few minutes later she burst from behind the double doors, crying.

"What's wrong?" I asked her.

"Nobody liked me."

"Oh, sure they did."

"No, they didn't. They didn't like my crown. They called me Smarty Pants!"

I almost said, I told you so. The words were on the tip of my tongue, ready to fly past my lips. Instead I said, "What makes them so smart? Wait till they hear you read."

"I did read. Then they called me *Smarty* Smarty Pants."

"Hey, Sam. If you stop crying, I'll let you help me with something."

She wiped her tears with the backs of her hands. "What?"

Just then, Mom pulled up in front of the school.

"Come on," I said. "I'll tell you on the way home."

9

The Fortune-Teller

Mom's bottom dresser drawer was filled with all kinds of scarves—a pink polka-dotted, a silk striped, a shiny black, a tiger print, and a green chiffon. Sam and Bruna watched close by as I pulled out each scarf. I found a long gold one that would be perfect for a head scarf.

Sam folded her arms across her chest. "I don't like that yucky color."

I swirled it around. "It's *gold*. Gold is mysterious."

Bruna snapped hold of the other end and tugged.

"No, Bruna."

To my surprise, she did.

"See?" I said. "Even Bruna likes the scarf."

"It looks like mustard."

"It's the only one long enough to wrap around your head."

"The tiger scarf is long enough," Sam said.

"Gypsy fortune-tellers don't wear tiger print."

"Do so!"

"Says who?"

"Says me, and I'm the Gypsy fortune-teller."

"Just for today." Just for the first official meeting of the Pensacola Gypsy Club. My Gypsy Club in San Diego hadn't been anywhere near this hard to start. The tree house had been enough. Now I had four kids from class coming over to get their fortunes told by my little sister, Sam. I'd thought about asking Tori, but she'd be mad at me for saying I knew a real Gypsy fortune-teller.

I was counting on Sam to convince my new friends. Sam stood still while I wrapped the gold scarf around her head. Then I pinned the scarf in place with bobby pins. After the last one was in, I stepped back to study Sam from head to toe. She looked like our great-aunt Sophie who had started to shrink and wore colorful turbans on her head.

Sam examined her reflection in the mirror, then stretched out her arms. "Presenting Madam God Bless America."

"Who?"

"Madam God Bless America."

"Sam, that's not a Gypsy name."

"Yes, it is."

"No, it's not. How about Madam Suranna or Madam Riccola?"

"No."

"Why do you want to be called Madam God Bless America? That's a song."

"It sounds important."

I sighed. "How about Madam America? That sounds important." I didn't like that either, but at least it didn't sound as ridiculous.

Sam put a finger to her temple. "Hmm. Okay!"

She slipped on my kimono. It was shiny blue with pink blossoms. I stood back and admired my work. Madam America didn't look that bad. Something was missing though.

"Where's my crystal ball?" Sam asked. "I have to have a crystal ball if I'm going to tell fortunes."

She was right. I rummaged around in the hall closet and the kitchen cabinets. A few minutes later I placed Mom's pink bowling ball on top of an upside-down dip bowl, making sure the finger holes were on the bottom. It kind of looked like a crystal ball.

Butterflies filled my insides. How would I ever convince my new friends with a five-year-old fortune-teller and a pink bowling ball? Then I realized that they'd probably never seen a fortune-teller anyway. How would they know what a real one looked like?

In my bedroom, I closed the blinds and plugged in the Donald Duck night-light. The night-light cast a yellow glow on the wall next to the TV tray, where I set the bowling ball and dip bowl.

Sam sat on a footstool behind the tray and only the top of the scarf could be seen. She was right. It did look like mustard. A puddle of mustard dripping off the TV tray. I switched the toy-box for the tray and threw a polka-dotted sheet over it. Sam sat cross-legged on the floor behind the box. That was much better.

When the doorbell rang, I jumped.

Mom called out, "Piper, your friends are here."

I went to the door. Hailey, Nicole, and Michael were waiting. "Where's Kami?" I asked.

"She didn't want to come," Michael said. "She doesn't believe you." Then he added, "I don't think I do either."

I was thankful that Mom didn't hear. She was already walking down the hall toward the kitchen. A rainbow of paint smudges covered her T-shirt.

"Is that the fortune-teller?" asked Hailey.

"Nah," I said. "Come on."

The kids followed me until we came to my room. I knocked at the closed door.

"You may enter," Sam called out in a deep voice I almost didn't recognize.

We tiptoed into my bedroom.

"Ooh," Nicole said.

"How cute!" Hailey said.

"Aw," said Michael. "She's just a little kid."

"She's a prodigy," I blurted, "a fortune-teller prodigy."

"Oh," Nicole said.

"Cool," said Hailey.

"Hmph," said Michael.

Stretching my arm toward Sam, I said, "May I present Madam America."

"Madam America?" Michael squinted. "Where are you from?"

"Iowa," Sam said.

Why couldn't she say someplace exotic? But I guess there aren't any Gypsy fortune-tellers in Europe named Madam America.

"What's the bowling ball for?" Michael asked.

I was afraid Michael might ruin the whole thing. I should have known that anyone who could touch his nose with his tongue and cross his eyes at the same time would be hard to fool.

"That's my crystal ball," Sam said.

Michael folded his arms across his chest. "Yeah, sure. The only thing that ball could tell you is how many gutters it's seen." .

"That's not nice, Michael," said Nicole. Then she asked, "Can I go first?"

"Sure," squeaked Sam. She dropped her voice. "I mean, sure."

Nicole settled in front of the toy box across from Sam. "What's my future, Madam America?"

Sam rubbed the bowling ball. It turned a bit and revealed the finger holes. "You're going to be very happy."

"Oh." Nicole smiled. "Thank you."

I could have kicked Sam. Why couldn't she say something more interesting, like "You're

going to break your leg" or "You're going to get
a part in the play"? We should have practiced
before they came over. But I studied Nicole. She
seemed to really believe Sam.

"Oh, brother," Michael said. "This is all fake."
Hailey twirled a lock of her red hair. "I want to
be next."

"Go ahead," I said, hoping Hailey would be as easy to please as Nicole.

Hailey sat, grinned, and waited while Sam rubbed the bowling ball.

"I see . . . I mean Madam America sees—"

"Yes?" Hailey leaned forward and stared at the finger holes in the bowling ball.

Sam frowned. "Madam America sees your future. You're going to be very sad."

"What?" Hailey jumped to her feet. "You are a fake, Piper. This isn't a real Gypsy fortune-teller."

"Am too," said Sam. "I'm Madam America."

Hailey headed toward the door. "I'm out of here."

"Me too," said Michael, following her.

Suddenly the door swung wide open. It took me a minute to recognize Tori. She wore Mom's long taffeta skirt and a peasant blouse hung low on her right shoulder. A gold earring dangled from one ear, and the tiger scarf surrounded her head. Her face looked three shades darker, but her neck and shoulders were still pale. Her bare feet stuck out from the skirt hem, and her silver baby ring circled her pinky toe.

"Hello, darlings," Tori purred in a foreign accent. "Does anyone want their fortune told?"

"Oh, brother," Michael groaned. "This is too weird."

I thought he was going to take off, but he didn't.

"Hey," Sam said, "I'm the fortune-teller."

"That's right, darling," purred Tori. "You're the fortune-teller-in-training. And you're doing an excellent job. I'm just here to finish your great start."

"Oh," said Sam. "Okay." She plopped on her bed and crossed her legs.

My head felt dizzy. How did Tori know? And

why was she helping me? Maybe she wasn't. Maybe she was going to make things worse. Everything was probably about to explode. If there wasn't so much stuff under my bed, I would have dived under there and taken cover.

"Young man," Tori said, facing Michael, "you seem to have your doubts."

"Oh, brother."

"May I read your future?"

"Why not?"

They settled across from each other on the floor. Sam pointed to the bowling ball. "There's the crystal ball."

"I don't need that." Tori took hold of Michael's chin and stared straight into his eyes. "Mmmhmm, just what I thought."

"What?" Michael asked.

"Success."

"Success?" Michael repeated.

"It's all around you."

"It is?" Michael was getting excited.

"Yes. Now if only you could touch it."

Michael wiggled. "Well, am I going to be successful?"

"Hold still," Tori said. "Madam Tova sees you are successful. Very successful."

"Am I going to be a famous basketball player?"

"No."

"Oh." Michael's shoulders sank. Why didn't Tori say he was going to be a famous basketball player? She was going to ruin this. She was going to give everyone fortunes they didn't want. Then they'd be mad at me and I wouldn't have any friends at my new school.

Tori leaned forward and caught hold of Michael's chin again. "Look at me. Madam Tova sees a gold medal being put around your neck."

"The Olympics?" Michael was excited again.

"Exactly," Tori said.

"Wow! What competition?"

"Surfing."

"Surfing? There's no surfing competition at the Olympics."

"There will be," Tori said.

"Cool. And I don't even own a surfboard."

Hailey raised her hand like she was in class.

Tori turned toward her. "Yes?"

"Madam America said I was going to be very sad."

Tori took hold of her chin. "That's right."

"I told you so," Sam said with a bounce.

Great! I thought, just when Tori was doing so well.

Tori leaned in close until she was an inch from Hailey's face. "You're going to lose a big diamond ring."

"Oh no!" Hailey said.

"But then you are going to find it and you become very, very happy. And rich."

Hailey smiled. "I knew it."

"How about you?" Tori asked Nicole.

"That's okay. Madam America said I was going to be happy."

A few minutes later their moms came and they

all left. But not before Michael asked, "When's the next meeting?"

"Next Saturday." Then I remembered that was when Chief would be leaving. "I mean next Sunday."

"Our mom is leaving Saturday," Nicole said.

"Yeah, on a ship," Michael added.

"So is our dad," I said. "He's sailing out on the USS *Julian*."

Michael and Nicole did a double take. "That's our mom's ship, too."

I smiled. Somehow knowing that Michael and Nicole would be missing their mom while I was missing Chief made them feel special, like good friends.

When they were gone I couldn't help myself. I gave Tori a great big hug.

She shrugged away. "Mush. What's that for?"

"For helping me and lying."

"I didn't lie, Piper. I was *pretending*."

"But I don't get it. How did you know?"

Tori pointed to the vent on the shared wall between our rooms. "There are no secrets in the Reed house."

But that wasn't true. There was one, and I'd never tell it. Tori Reed would never know that I thought she was the best big sister in the whole wide world.

10

FIELD TRIP

My class lined up to get on the bus for our field trip. I couldn't wait to see the Blue Angels up close. I hurried to the front of the line because that way I could be on the very top bleacher. I'd be closer to the sky and closer to the Blue Angels.

Michael headed toward the back of the line.

"Where are you going?" I called out.

He didn't hear me, so I stepped out of line to ask him.

"I like to sit at the back of the bus," he

said. "I can make faces at the cars following us."

"But if you go to the front you can sit on the top bleacher."

He shrugged. "So what?"

"Don't you want to get the best seat?"

Michael scowled. "It's the sky. We'll be looking at the sky."

I left him and walked to the front of the line.

Shelby Snodgrass scooted closer to know-it-all-raise-her-hand-for-every-question Kami. "You can't cut," Shelby said.

"I'm not. I was here a second ago."

"Too bad," Kami said. "You got out of line."

"But I'm back," I insisted.

Kami's hands flew to her hips. "You should have said, 'Save my place, please.'"

"That's right, Piper," said Shelby.

Ms. Gordon walked over to us. "Is there a problem here?"

"Piper is trying to cut in line," Kami said.

"Yep, that's right," said Shelby.

Ms. Gordon took a deep breath. "Sorry, Piper. You'll have to go to the back of the line. Don't worry. We're not going to leave anyone behind."

"But—"

Ms. Gordon's eye began to twitch. She should probably see a doctor about that. It always seemed to happen when she talked to me. "Piper, we have to hurry if we're going to make it to practice on time."

I went to the back of the line. I was sure glad Kami didn't want to be in our Gypsy Club.

When I reached the end, Michael shook his head. "The Blue Angels will be in the sky. There won't be a bad view."

On the bus, Michael and I sat in the very last seat and made faces at the cars behind us all the way to the base. When we got there, we passed the jet in front of the Blue Angels headquarters.

Everyone on the bus clapped. "Yea!"

A man who worked for the Blue Angels met the bus, and we followed him to the airfield until we reached the bleachers. Michael and I sat on the bottom bleacher with the other pokey kids at the end of the line.

Hailey and Nicole sat on the middle bleacher. Nicole was frowning. Earlier she told me she didn't want to go on the field trip. She'd said, "I get migraines from loud noises and nauseous from having to look at the sky."

By the time our class settled on the bleachers, the Blue Angel pilots had lined up. Slowly, one at a time, they rode past us and waved.

Everyone waved back, but I swung my arm so wide that I hit Michael in the ear.

"Hey, watch it," he said.

"Sorry."

One at a time, they took off, soaring into the air.

"Get off the bus!" I yelled.

No one could hear me, because the jets' roar was so loud.

The Blue Angels flipped, they crisscrossed, they pointed their noses straight up like rockets.

I made up a name for each trick. "That's a split-air spiral," I told Michael.

"What?" he yelled.

"A split-air spiral."

Just then, two jets looked as if they were going to crash into each other, but a second later, one leaned toward the right and the other toward the left.

"Get off the bus!" hollered Michael. That was the first time he'd said that. He really was an official Gypsy Club member.

I glanced behind me. Nicole's hands covered

her ears and she was closing her eyes. How could she miss such an exciting moment? I should make it a Gypsy Club rule that every member must carefully watch the Blue Angels. They shouldn't even blink. I turned toward Michael. He blinked. I quickly changed my mind about the rule.

Smoke scribbled the sky. I imagined the streams spelling "Piper Reed."

Practice was over too soon. Just as they had taken off, the pilots landed one by one. Then the announcer introduced them. When he called out the last pilot, he said, "Lieutenant Commander Elizabeth Franklin."

"Lieutenant Commander Elizabeth," I repeated. And in that moment, I knew exactly what I was going to be when I grew up. Piper Reed: Blue Angel.

We lined up again, this time to have our class picture taken with the flying team. When it was

our turn to stand in front of the jet with the team, I pushed ahead of Kami to be next to Lieutenant Commander Franklin.

"Hey," Kami said. "You're cutting."

But before she could catch Ms. Gordon's attention, I told Lieutenant Commander Franklin,

"I'm going to be a Blue Angel when I grow up."

She smiled. "That's super! First, you've got to work hard in school and read a lot of books."

Standing by the Navy photographer, Ms. Gordon mouthed, *Thank you.* Teachers always got excited when adults said things like that.

As we headed toward the bus, I swung around and saluted Lieutenant Commander Franklin. I wondered if she even noticed. But a second later, she raised her hand and saluted me back!

11

CAPTAIN PIPER REED

Monday night, Tori chose Chinese food and then some dumb movie for her special time with Chief.

The next night was Sam's turn. She chose McDonald's, the zoo, and a pet store. When they returned home, Sam held up a plastic bag so I could get a close-up view of the shiny goldfish swimming back and forth.

"Daddy says it can be all mine."

"Fine," I told her. "I don't want a stupid gold-fish anyway."

She raced down the hall with her goldfish sloshing to and fro. Before going into our room, she swung around and said, "I named her Peaches."

For days, I had tried to think of a special place that Chief could take me. But after my field trip, I knew what I wanted to do. Wednesday after-noon, Chief picked me up from school so we could go to the Naval Aviation Museum.

We walked into the museum ahead of a group of old people. The men wore blue hats that said U.S. NAVY or RETIRED VET above the bills.

I'd never seen so many jets and airplanes inside a building. I closed my eyes and pictured myself flying them. I wore a uniform just like Lieutenant Commander Elizabeth Franklin. I was approaching

the clouds when I heard my name. "Captain Piper Reed."

"Piper?" Chief put his hand on my arm. "I've called your name three times. You must have been a million miles away."

"I was listening for my orders."

"What?" Chief looked confused.

"Nothing."

"How would you like to see a movie about the Blue Angels?"

"Yes, sir."

Five minutes later we were sitting in the museum's IMAX theater, watching the Blue Angels train and fly their jets. A pilot in the film said Blue Angels were Navy pilots first and foremost. That even though they loved performing, they couldn't wait to return to flying for the Navy.

The best part was when the jet landed on a Navy carrier. Even before they showed what happened next, I knew. The aviation mechanics would check out the jets to make sure everything was okay. I knew that, since Chief was an aviation mechanic. I turned around to the audience and shouted, "That's what my dad does!"

After the museum and film, we drove off-base to Pensacola Beach to eat dinner at the Seafood Grill. The hostess sat us next to a big window that overlooked the Gulf. A few minutes later a waiter came over with our menus. "Pretty young lady you got there," he said.

"Yes, she is," said Chief. "Got three more just like her at home."

"Lucky man," the waiter said, before walking away.

But I wasn't just like Tori, and I wasn't anything like Sam or Mom either. I was nothing like them. Why couldn't Chief see that?

After I ordered popcorn shrimp and french fries, I announced, "I'm going to be a Blue Angel when I grow up."

Chief's face broke into a big grin. "Is that right?"

"I'm serious."

Chief stopped smiling. "I believe you, Piper."

"You do?"

"Sure, I do. You've always done what you've set your mind on. You walked when you were nine months old. We'd try to help you, but you'd push our hands away."

My popcorn shrimp arrived on a plate with a mountain of french fries. Outside the window, the water glistened as the sun sank below the horizon. My chest filled up and my shoulders straightened. I was going to be in the U.S. Navy, just like Chief. Only I'd fly the blue skies and do flips through the clouds. Then, when I landed on the carrier, Chief and the other mechanics would rush over and check my jet.

We stared out the window. Chief and I laughed when a seagull landed on one of the tables, snatched a woman's roll, then flew away.

On the drive home, Chief headed in the opposite direction from the base.

"Where are you going?" I asked.

"You'll see."

Chief drove until we came to a store's parking lot outside the commercial airfield. He turned off the engine and rolled down the windows. The sky was dark except for the lights that lit the runway. We watched a jet take off. The roar shook our van. It almost felt like we were inside a jet.

"Just think," Chief said. "That will be you one day. We'll point to the sky and say, 'There she goes, Lieutenant Piper Reed.'"

"Lieutenant? How about Captain?"

Chief laughed. "Captain Piper Reed, you are an original."

12

SEE YOU LATER, ALLIGATOR

We stood in the front yard waving good-bye to Chief. I wondered if Michael and Nicole were saying good-bye to their mom at that exact moment. Tomorrow was our second Gypsy Club meeting, and I had no idea what we'd be doing. Somehow, it didn't matter.

One of Chief's co-workers had picked him up in a jeep to take him to the airport. The jeep was halfway down our cul-de-sac when Sam hollered, "See you later, alligator!"

I swallowed, trying to push down the lump in my throat. "He can't hear you."

But just then, Chief turned, waved real big, and called back, "In a while, crocodile!"

Sam jumped up and down. "He heard me! He heard me! He heard me!"

"How long will Chief be gone?" I asked.

Mom brushed a lock of hair from her eyes. "Six months." She said the words so softly they almost came out in a whisper.

"Six months is a long time," Tori said.

"It takes *nine* months to make a baby," said Sam.

Mom's right eyebrow shot up. "How do you know that?"

Sam sighed. "Agatha Waynewright told me. She knows everything."

I smirked. "I thought *you* knew everything."

"Not like Agatha," Sam said.

"What else does Agatha know?" Mom asked.

"That there's really not any vanilla in vanilla ice cream and that the reason kids have bedtimes is because their parents are sick of them and need a break."

Mom gave Sam a big squeeze. "I'm not sick of you." Then she hugged me. "Nor you." Then she caught hold of Tori's wrist and pulled her toward her. "Nor you either." She took a deep breath and added, "Your dad will be home before we know it. Meanwhile, why don't you walk over to the store and get Popsicles?"

"By ourselves?" I asked.

"If one of you holds Sam's hand. And if you watch out for cars."

Normally I would have said, "Get off the bus!" but I didn't feel like it.

Tori grabbed Sam's hand. "I'll hold her hand on the way there. You can hold it on the way back." She was so bossy.

We left our street and passed the officers' housing and the chapel. I could hear a jet flying above us, but I didn't bother to look. Soon we reached the little store that was near the school where Chief would teach when he got back from ship duty.

At the store, we opened the freezer that held ice cream and Popsicles. There were all kinds of

flavors—strawberry, orange, cherry, lime. But all three of us chose grape. We'd never done that before. We always liked to choose something different.

Before we left the store, we threw away the wrappers. We hadn't been walking two minutes when I let go of Sam's hand. "Yuk! Your fingers are sticky!"

Sam burst into tears. "I can't help it! Daddy always wipes them for me with his handkerchief."

The lump in my throat grew bigger.

"You made her cry," Tori snapped.

"I didn't mean to," I said.

I grabbed Sam's sticky fingers. "It's okay. They're not that bad."

By the time we arrived home, we were almost finished with our Popsicles. The yellow sprinkler was shooting water around the yard. A little spongy ball was on the dry part of the grass, just beyond the sprinkler's reach. Some neighbor must have dropped it there.

Mom had left her radio playing on the porch steps, and we settled next to it while we finished our treats.

Sam stuck out her tongue. "I bet my tongue is purple."

"Yeah," I said, "so is mine."

"But mine is purplier," Sam said.

"How do you know?" I asked. "You can't even see it."

Mom cracked the door open. Her cheeks were rosy and her voice sounded excited. "Girls, we've already received an e-mail from your dad. He said he arrived at the airport and realized he hadn't given us the new bathroom assignment list. Karl and his lists!"

She laughed so hard that two giant tears rolled

down her cheeks. "Oh yes, he also said, 'I already miss my girls!'"

Mom went back inside, but not before Bruna slipped through the narrow opening. Bruna sat next to us on the steps. She looked like she was waiting for something important to happen.

Bruna followed as I walked over to the ball. After she sniffed it, I threw the ball to the other side of the yard. "Fetch!"

Bruna took off after it, her little ears flopping the whole way.

Something inside me soared. "Look, Bruna does tricks, just like Kip!"

She picked up the ball with her mouth.

My heart pounded. "Come here, Bruna. Bring it here!"

But Bruna ignored me and ran around the yard with the ball, dashing through the stream of water. I should have known better than to get my hopes up. At least she knew half of a trick.

"Hey, listen!" Tori turned up the volume on the radio. "Johnny B. Goode" poured out from

the speaker. It was as if Chief was sending his favorite song our way.

And then, without even discussing it, all three of us picked up our Popsicle sticks and sang into them. Our voices cracked the words as we danced around the yard, darting in and out of the sprinkler's aim. We probably looked silly to anyone who happened to be staring out the window, watching us sing and dance as we got our clothes drenched. But to us, it was magic——sister magic.

That night I took out a piece of paper and started a list. I didn't know how to spell all the words, but everything on the list was true.

ThiNGS I LiKE ABOUT LiViNG iN PENSaCOLa

1. Pensacola is the home of the Blue Angels.
2. We can walk to the beach.
3. I started a new Gypsy Club.

4. We have a dog named Bruna who can do tricks (sort of).
5. Ms. Mitchell thinks I'm a pleasure.
6. Pensacola is where we'll be when Chief comes back to us.
7. Sometimes (when Tori is not too bossy and Sam is not such a smarty pants), it's fun to have sisters who like grape Popsicles the best, too.
8. I have now spread "Get off the bus" to another state. There are only 48 more to go!

KIMBERLY WILLIS HOLT

is the author of several award-winning novels, including *My Louisiana Sky*; *Keeper of the Night*; *Part of Me;* and *When Zachary Beaver Came to Town*, which received the National Book Award for Young People's Literature. She has also written the picture books *Waiting for Gregory* and *Skinny Brown Dog*.

A former Navy brat herself, Ms. Holt lived all over the world as a child and now resides in west Texas with her family.

www.kimberlywillisholt.com

CHRISTINE DAVENIER

has illustrated many books for young readers, such as *The First Thing My Mama Told Me*, which was a *New York Times* Best Illustrated Book, as well as *Leon and Albertine*. She lives in Paris, France, with her daughter, Josephine.

QUESTIONS FOR THE AUTHOR

KIMBERLY WILLIS HOLT

What did you want to be when you grew up?
A writer.

When did you realize you wanted to be a writer?
In seventh grade, three teachers encouraged my writing. That was when I first thought the dream could come true. Before that, I didn't think I could be a writer because I wasn't a great student and I read slowly.

What's your first childhood memory?
Buying an orange Dreamsicle from the ice-cream man. I was two years old.

What's your most embarrassing childhood memory?
In fourth grade, I tried to impress the popular girls that I wanted to be friends with by doing somersaults in front of them. (I never learned to do cartwheels.) They called me a showoff, so I guess it didn't work. If only I'd known how to do a cartwheel.

What was your worst subject in school?
Algebra.

What was your first job?
I was in the movies. I popped popcorn at the Westside Cinemas.

How did you celebrate publishing your first book?
I'm sure my family went out to dinner. We always celebrate by eating.

Where do you write your books?
I write several places—a soft, big chair in my bedroom, at a table on my screen porch, or at coffee shops.

Where do you find inspiration for your writing?
Most of the inspiration for my writing comes from moments in my childhood.

Which of your characters is most like you?
I'm a bit like most of them. However, I fashioned Tori in the Piper Reed books after me. But Tori is bossier than I was and she certainly makes better grades than I did.

When you finish a book, who reads it first?
My daughter listens to me read my first draft.

Are you a morning person or a night owl?
I'm a morning person.

What's your idea of the best meal ever?
That's a toss-up. My grandmother's chicken and dumplings, and sushi.

Which do you like better: cats or dogs?
I'm a dog person. I have a poodle named Bronte who is the model for Bruna.

What do you value most in your friends?
Loyalty and honesty.

Where do you go for peace and quiet?
Home.

Who is your favorite fictional character?
Leroy in *Mister and Me* because he is forgiving. And that's a trait many of us don't have.

What are you most afraid of?
Anything harming my daughter.

What time of the year do you like best?
Fall.

What is your favorite TV show?
CBS Sunday Morning.

If you were stranded on a desert island, who would you want for company?
My husband and daughter.

What's the best advice you have ever received about writing?

A writer once told me, "Readers either see what they read or hear what they read. Writers have to learn to write for both." When I started following that advice, my writing improved.

What do you want readers to remember about your books?

The characters. I want them to seem like real people. I want them to miss them and wonder what happened to them.

What would you do if you ever stopped writing?

I plan on dying with a pen in my hand.

What do you like best about yourself?

I'm honest.

What is your worst habit?

I eat too much.

What do you consider to be your greatest accomplishment?

I gave birth to a wonderful human being.

What do you wish you could do better?

I wish I could do a cartwheel.

What would your readers be most surprised to learn about you?

I send gift cards with positive messages to myself when I order something for me.

*K*eep reading for an excerpt from
Piper Reed: The Great Gypsy,
available now in hardcover from Henry Holt.

EXCERPT

My little sister, Sam, knelt on the sofa, staring out the window. Our next-door neighbors moved off base last week, and she was watching for our new neighbors to arrive.

That's the way the Navy life was. Someone was always coming and someone was always going. Before we moved to Pensacola, we'd lived in California, Texas, Guam, Mississippi, and New Hampshire. Just when a place started to feel like home, we had to leave, again.

"The moving van is here!" Sam called out.

Tori and I rushed over to the window. My older sister was twelve and boy crazy. She probably wanted some goofy guy to move next door so that she could flutter her eyelashes at him. I was hoping for a fourth-grader, another potential Gypsy Club member. I started the Gypsy Club when we lived in San Diego. I'd already recruited three members while in Pensacola.

"I hope there's a five-year-old girl, just like me, moving in," said Sam. She leaned to the far right, stretching her neck as if she expected a kindergartner to pop out of the van.

I pointed to Sam's reflection in the window. "There she is."

"Where?"

"Right there. She looks exactly like you."

When Sam caught on, she stuck out her chin. "I'm not stupid."

"I know. You're a prodigy—a spelling bee prodigy."

Tori gave me a shove with her elbow. "Move over, Piper. You're hogging all the space, and I can't see."

"You just take up more room," I told her. When I wanted to get back at Tori, I mentioned her chubby body.

Tori's face turned purple. "You're mean, Piper Reed!"

She was right. Since Chief left, I'd said something mean every day. That meant I'd said seven mean things because seven days had passed since our dad left for ship duty.

A big calendar hung on our kitchen wall with a red X crossed through each day. Chief would be gone six long months. Each day we took turns marking off another day. Even Mom got a turn. In the Reed household we took turns for everything. And that means I'm always in the middle because *I am* the middle.

Mom handed the marker to me. "Go ahead, Piper. It's your turn."

"Why do I always have to be last?" Sam asked as I marked an X over November 11. I guess there were worse things than being in the middle. At least I wasn't Sam who would always be the baby of the family, even when she was ninety-five years old.

"It can be fun to be last," Tori told Sam. "Haven't you heard 'Save the best for last'?"

"That's easy for you to say," I said. "You're always first."

Sam fixed her hands on her hips. "Well, I'm going to be the first one to kiss Daddy when he gets off the ship."

Mom sighed, but she wasn't paying any attention to us. She stood at the kitchen table, looking over her paint box. Monday she'd start teaching art at our school. That's when our art teacher, Mrs. Kimmel, goes on maternity leave. School would be weird having Mom there. I hoped she wouldn't ask me in front of the class if I remembered to brush my teeth.

"What about papier-mâché?" Mom asked, thumbing through newspaper scraps.

"We did papier-mâché piggy banks last week," I said. "Remember?"

Mom made a snapping noise with her tongue. "Oh, yeah. Drats!"

"Why can't they do papier-mâché again?" Tori asked.

"I want the students to make something different."

"You could let us have recess during art," I suggested.

Tori scowled. "Why would she do that?"

I shrugged. "Well, that would be different."

"We didn't do papier-mâché," said Sam.

"You didn't?" Mom sounded excited.

"Mom," I said, "think about it. Twenty kinder-gartners with a bunch of mush and newspaper strips? They would be a disaster."

"Oh," she said. "Good point."

Sam looked offended. "No, we won't."

"Piper is right," Mom said.

Sam frowned at me. "You spoil everything!"

"Sam, you could handle it," said Mom, "but so many of your other classmates wouldn't be able to create papier-mâché without making a huge mess."

Sam straightened her back. "That's true."

Great, I thought. Sam, the prodigy. Sam, who

could read better than me, and now I couldn't even count on her to make a big mess with papier-mâché.

Mom turned off the pot of beans on the stove. They'd been cooking all day, and the smell of sausage and onions filled our kitchen.

Grabbing her sketchbook, Mom said, "We'll eat dinner soon, but first I'm going to take a bath. Creative ideas always come to me in the tub."

"Like a think tank?" Sam asked.

Mom smiled. "Yes, I guess you could say that."

Maybe I'd take a long soak later because I needed a good idea, too. I wanted to accomplish something fantastic so Chief would be extra proud of me when he returned.

I walked over to the computer. "I'll check our e-mail to see if Chief wrote to us yet."

Tori and Sam followed me.

Every day Chief e-mailed us. Sometimes there was a message waiting in the morning. Sometimes it was there after school. But no matter what, a message was there every day. We could count on it.

Dear Girls,
  I've only been gone a week and already it feels like a year. But that's because it's the first

*week. The time will pass quickly, just wait
and see. But don't grow too much. I won't
recognize you.*

*By the way, I forgot to tell you a few things.
Make sure you print the attachment and put it
on the refrigerator.*

That could mean only one thing. We opened the
attachment.

"Great," Tori muttered when a list appeared.

1. Sweep the porch every afternoon.
2. Rake the yard once a month.
3. Wash the car at least every other Saturday.
  Don't forget the tire rims.

Chief didn't need a think tank to make lists. He
could make one anytime—while he ate a Big Mac
or watched TV or stretched out on the couch. Mom
called it his hobby, but I think it's because you have
to know how to make lists when you're a chief in the
U.S. Navy.

A few minutes later, Sam called out, "They're here!
The new neighbors are here!"

The three of us raced outside. I decided I wouldn't mind if there was a bratty girl Sam's age or a goofy boy Tori's age, as long as there was someone my age. Someone who could become an official Gypsy Club member and say "Get off the bus!" when they were excited. It was my goal to spread that saying around the world, and I'd already spread it to California and Florida.

A blue car had parked next door. A second later, a man got out from behind the driver's seat and then his wife opened the passenger door. The lady smiled at us.

I wasn't sure of their rank, but I saluted them anyway. "Hi. Welcome to NAS Pensacola, home of the Blue Angels!"

The man's face broke out into a big grin. He even had dimples.

Tori elbowed me. "What are you? The welcome committee?"

"That's a lovely welcome," the lady said. "My name is Yolanda and this is Abe."

"Good to meet you," Abe said. "I guess the people in Florida are as warm as the climate."

They seemed nice, but where were their kids? Maybe their kids were grown. But Yolanda and Abe looked too young for that. Maybe they didn't have any kids. My shoulders sank.

Then Yolanda opened the car's back door and ducked her head inside. I heard her say, "Come on, Brady. Don't be shy."

Brady? That could be a girl or a boy. That could be a five-year-old, or a twelve-year-old, or maybe a nine-year-old. That could be a future Gypsy Club member.

But a moment later Yolanda straightened and in her ams was a little kid. A *big* little kid. Almost the same size as Sam.

Yolanda kissed the top of his head. "This is Brady. He's two years old. He's kind of tall for his age."

Brady held out three fingers. "Twee!" he said.

"You have a good ways to go before you're three," Yolanda said, smiling.

We stood there, studying Brady. He had dimples just like Abe. None of us said a word. Then Bruna walked over to them and wagged her tail.

Brady pointed to her, bouncing on his mother's hip. "Dog!" he said.

Great, I thought. Just what I need—another child prodigy!